For Cameron, who loves stories
~ A M

For Miłosz and Mateusz
~ M B

LITTLE TIGER PRESS LTD,
an imprint of the Little Tiger Group
1 Coda Studios, 189 Munster Road,
London SW6 6AW
www.littletiger.co.uk
First published in Great Britain 2019
Text copyright © Alan MacDonald 2019
Illustrations copyright © Magda Brol 2019

Alan MacDonald and Magda Brol have asserted
their rights to be identified as the author and illustrator of this
work under the Copyright, Designs and Patents Act, 1988

PiRATES DON'T GO TO SCHOOL!

Alan MacDonald

Magda Brol

LiTTLE TiGER
LONDON

On the *Salty Prawn*, the pirates were busy.
"Swab the poop deck!" hollered Pa.
"Scrape them barnacles!" shouted Ma.
"Mend the mainsail!" cried Gran.
"And where's my tea, Jake?"
But Jake was tired of mopping parrot poop.
"Pa, when can I go to school?" he sighed.

"SCHOOL?" gasped his family. "Pirates don't go to school!"
"School is hard and horrible!" growled Pa.
"It's all rotten work and rotten rules," muttered Ma.
"And teachers is mean as sea monsters!" warned Gran.
But Jake longed to go and he kept on asking.

"All right, all right, we surrender!" groaned Pa. "YOU CAN GO TO BLOOMIN' SCHOOL!"

At sunrise, Jake's family rowed him ashore. He had a ship's biscuit from Ma, and Poll the parrot hidden under his hat.

"Poor little sprat!" sniffled Gran. "I hope he'll be all right."

The playground was HUGE.
Jake stood all by himself, feeling
very small.

"What if my teacher *is* a terrible,
ten-legged sea monster?" he worried.

Suddenly a giant shadow loomed
over him. Jake gulped . . .

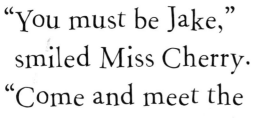

"You must be Jake," smiled Miss Cherry. "Come and meet the class!"

"Ahoy there, mates," said Jake, raising his hat politely. But he'd forgotten what was underneath! Poll woke up with a screech and took off.

ARK!

"Good heavens!" gasped Miss Cherry.
"Oh no!" cried Jake. "Come back,
you pesky parrot, come back!"

They chased Poll into the hall where a gym lesson was in full swing.

"Heave-ho, mates," cried Jake. "I've got her cornered."

Quick as a monkey, he climbed up a rope. But Poll didn't wait to be caught.

"Oh dear!" sighed Miss Cherry.
"Blow me down!" moaned Jake.

Outside, Jake hunted high and low.

"Where's that feather-brained bird gone now?" he sighed.

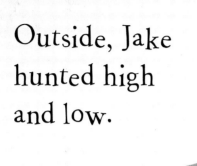

"There she is!" cried a girl. "Look out!"

The headteacher hit the deck as Poll swooped low across the playground.

"Sink me!" groaned Jake. "What now?"

But then he had an idea!

Taking out his biscuit, he broke
off some crumbs.

"Hey, Poll, look what I've got!"
he called.

Poll's eyes shone greedily; ship's
biscuits were her favourite. With
a squawk, she took off . . .

Poll wants
a cracker!

. . . and landed neatly on Jake's hand.
"Thank heavens!" sighed
Miss Cherry.
"HOORAY!" cheered the class.
"That pesky parrot came back!"

Who's a clever Poll then?

Jake knew he was in BIG trouble.
Pesky parrots were sure to be
against the rotten rules.
    Miss Cherry folded her arms.
"Well, Jake, what should we do now?"
    "Send me home?" mumbled Jake.

Miss Cherry laughed. "I've got a much better idea. Who likes singing?"

"ME!" shouted Jake, because singing is one thing pirates love best.

"Pots and brushes out, time to do some painting!" said Miss Cherry. "Follow me, mates!" cried Jake, because pirates love to make a sploshy mess.

By story time, Jake had forgotten his worries about the rotten rules and getting into trouble. He listened to Miss Cherry read a tale about treasure buried deep on Parrot Island. Even Poll seemed to like it.

At home time, Jake's family stood waiting at the gates.

"Well, lad?" they said.

"Was school hard and horrible?"

"NO!" cried Jake.
"I WANT TO GO AGAIN!"

And he told them all about his day.

"Well boil me bedsocks!" cried Pa.

"It sounds like one bloomin' big adventure.
Maybe school is for pirates after all!"
So the next day when Jake went back . . .

. . . he brought along his
whole bloomin' family!

Sea
creatures